Four Twisted Dreams

Taila Cantrell

Contents

Dedication   IV

Trigger Warnings   V

1. Chapter 1   1

2. Chapter 2   8

3. Chapter 3   12

4. Chapter 4   17

5. Chapter 5   23

6. Chapter 6   29

7. Chapter 7   37

8. Chapter 8   44

9. Chapter 9   49

10. Chapter 10   54

Epilogue   58

Acknowledgements   62

About the author   63

Also by   64

Dedication

For those of you who have been shamed into believing you are not beautiful, powerful, and wonderful. Don't let the words of others dull your shine.

Trigger Warnings

Child Abuse

Somnophilia

Homophobia

Murder

DVP

Arson

BDSM- Please keep in mind that this is a work of fiction. If you are interested in practicing BDSM please keep it safe, sane, and consensual.

One

This dreamscape was more peaceful than the ones I usually landed in. I'd lost count of how many years Harris had kept me trapped away from the coven, feeding me strange potions and forcing me into a constant dream state.

"Aislinn?" A soft voice asked from behind me. I turned to find a stunning redhead dressed in white watching me carefully. I opened my mouth to respond, but I couldn't find the words, "It's okay. My name is Xava. Everett sent me here to speak to you."

The emotions that welled in my chest were more than I could take. For the first few months I'd been entranced, I'd tried to hunt for Everett, but the first time Harris caught me... Well, let's say it hadn't been worth looking anymore. Some part of myself still had self-preservation. I may have given up on my dreams many years ago, but some part of me desperately wanted to stay alive even if there was only a slim chance of ever having freedom. "This is a cruel trick to play, Harris. After all of the years you've tortured me with visions of Everett dead." I summoned enough energy to sass the illusion he'd provided me.

The redhead cracked a smile, "I respect the doubt, sister. Everett, though you might be unsure of me, we couldn't risk him being the one to do this. He said to tell you that Mr. Moo is still alive and chewing on his shoes anytime he's given the opportunity."

My blood ran cold. There was no way for Harris to know about the tiny cat I'd snuck into the coven compound when Everett and I were children. He would have ensured that the cat was killed in front of me to fuel his torment. At the same time, I knew there was no chance... Unless. I took a deep breath, closing my eyes and finding the small light inside of myself that I'd hidden away years ago. The light that had always made me believe that Harris's visions were a lie. As soon as I ran my hand over our bond, I knew the truth. It hummed as I reopened my eyes. "Why are you here?"

"Everett is close to your location, but a powerful spell is preventing him and my bonded from getting you out. We need you to help us." Xava explained, "I don't know the conditions you're being kept in, but if you could try to find and work against the spell, we may be able to get to you faster."

My heart plummeted. There was no way I was going to be able to help the way that she expected. My magic was drained. I couldn't light a match if I was going to freeze to death. I knew that from experience. "I can't help."

Xava hummed, showing no signs of irritation. Instead, she paced for a moment, her form flickering slightly. "Everett says he knows who is holding you. All we need you to do is find a way to keep him distracted for fifteen minutes."

"When? There's no way for us to communicate." I knew the frustration growing inside me shouldn't be directed at the woman before me, but I couldn't help the way I felt. "It's hopeless. He shouldn't risk being harmed."

Xava moved toward me, a sense of comfort filled me as she wrapped her arms around me. It was the closest I'd come to kind contact in so long that I broke down immediately. "Have faith in the Mother and Father, Aislinn. They do not want bonds kept apart."

Xava said before pulling away, "Hold on tight to your bond with Everett and trust your instincts. You'll know when."

I felt the loss of her comfort when she moved away. Her mouth opened, but whatever she was going to say was lost as I was hurled out of the dreamscape.

My eyes flew open as a bucket of ice-cold water splashed over me. I gasped for air, unable to stop my body from reacting to the stinging pain in my skin.

"Up and change into the clothes on the table. Harris will be dining with you this afternoon." The bark of the guard made my ears ring. At least he didn't try to touch me like the last one.

I moved slowly into a sitting position, glancing at the black dress that had been laid on the table. I hated it. He knew I hated the color black; it made me look dead. I guess that's what he loved about it. If I died, he wouldn't be forced to deal with me any longer. The greatest shame to the Dream Coven, the bastard daughter with the strange eyes and the gay bond. My father did so pride himself on our family history. My great-great-great-great-grandfather had been the first Dream witch to form a Coven in the United States of America. It was not true, of course. There had been Native American Covens here hundreds, if not thousands, of years before Old Grandad Richard started one. Harris didn't believe that to be true.

I sighed, forcing myself to stand. Every inch of my body ached as I stripped off the pale-yellow night gown I wore. It was stained and gross, so at least the water would make it a little cleaner. If I were lucky, someone would bring me a bar of soap soon. I had kept the scraps of my last bar going as long as I could, but it was almost gone.

I pulled the black dress over my head. It swallowed my thin frame, hanging off my body in a way that made me feel sick. I had always been thin, but never to this point. My collarbones jutted out now. I wasn't getting enough food to stay alive. It had gotten worse over the years. Harris visited less and less. When he'd found that he could torture me from a distance, he'd been overjoyed; he got to spend more time with his perfect little coven. While still ensuring that I stayed locked away so that I could never bring shame to his name again. I sat at the small table, rolling over the dream in my mind until I was dizzy from the panic. I couldn't be certain that it wasn't a normal dream. I still had them occasionally. This had seemed different, though, more real. I could feel the bond in my chest more than I had in a very long time. It pulsed in time with my heartbeat.

I felt magic leak into the room before Harris had even opened the door. I braced myself for the images that flashed through my mind, horrible, unspeakable things that forced my body to freeze. I was locked in those images long enough for him to sit and have food brought into the room without my knowledge.

"Evening, wretch. Dan tells me you've been less of a bother this last couple of months. Since you've decided to have a modicum of decency with your keepers, I had some of your favorites brought in. When he pulled the cover back from the plate, I forced myself not to recoil. The plate was filled with bacon. Once upon a time, bacon had been one of my favorite foods, I could have eaten it for every meal. Until Harris ensured to send me nightmares involving disgusting scenarios. I may have felt sick at the idea of eating it, but I knew I'd have no choice. Either I'd eat it willingly, or Harris would have it force-fed to me.

"Thank you," I replied primly. I tucked the napkin provided onto my lap, knowing Harris would punish any perceived lack of etiquette.

We stared at each other for a long moment before he scoffed, putting various foods on his plate. I waited for him to begin eating before I took a few small pieces of each item he'd offered. I took small bites, eating them slowly until my stomach cramped. Thankfully, my plate was empty when I began to feel sick.

"I have fantastic news," Harris said, clapping his hands together. "Cierra has found her bonded. In just a few months, she'll ascend to her rightful spot as Priestess in training."

It was rare to find your bond before turning twenty-five, almost unheard of, actually. Cierra was my half-sister, the child of Harris and the coven's Priestess. They weren't bonded, but they got along well enough. Eva was nicer than Harris, had occasionally snuck me small treats when I was young. "Congratulations," I said, ensuring to keep my voice upbeat. I didn't want to make him angry with me tonight.

"Once she's ascended, I will have more time to work on our spell." He responded. I nearly choked on my water. I had hoped he'd given up the stupid plan he had cooked up, had decided to keep me here for fun. "Yes, I think in just a few months we will finally be able to find the missing piece." I zoned out at that. Whatever he rambled on about was white noise to my ears as my mind wandered to his spell. He believed that a dream witch could enter the realm of the Mother and Father. He was set on being the warlock to prove the theory. I had fought against his plans at every turn. Astral projection was one of my strongest gifts. That was the real reason he kept me locked up here. If the Coven knew what I could do, if they saw the mark on my brow from my ascension, his perfect little world would crumble. I had daydreamed about that life many times before, but I knew the truth. Harris would kill me before he let me out. I would never see my bond again and I would certainly never become Priestess. So long as I lived, though, Harris would never complete his spell. I would not allow him to disturb our gods. The Mother and Father blessed me with the only happiness I experienced in my short, miserable life. I wouldn't let my father disrespect them. A sharp blow to my face brought me out of my quiet musings, "You will listen when I'm speaking to you." Harris howled as he reared back to hit me again.

Something was different this time, maybe my strange dream had awoken me from my submission or maybe the reality that he would pass off Cierra as Priestess of the Dream coven was too much. I caught his hand, catching him off guard enough that I was able to slip behind him. I wrapped my arm around his neck, "I will never complete your spell. You might as well kill me." I hissed.

He gasped, trying to respond, but the sounds of alarms drowned out his words. A tug in my gut had me losing my grip. He slammed me into the concrete wall, forcing the air from my lungs. I crumpled to the floor gasping for breath. Harris leaned down, gripping long strands of my tangled hair, "You are nothing, Aislinn. You will rot and die in these four walls while my true daughter brings the Dream coven to new heights. You will help with my spell, or I will call on some my friends to extract your powers. I'm sure they would have a very good time with you."

Before I could respond the door swung open, smacking into my legs, "Sir, we're under attack. I've come to get you out of the building safely."

"Under attack? No one knows this place even exists." He growled. With a final kick to my ribs Harris allowed the guard to escort him out. I heard the lock on the door click shut. They were going to abandon me to whoever was attacking the building.

I couldn't let myself hope that my dream had been real. That the tug in my chest now was anything more than the figment of my imagination. A fiction my broken mind has created to cope with the horrors of my life here.

The next thing I knew I was being lifted into strong arms. I didn't have the strength to fight off whoever carried me, but as I cracked my eyes open, I flinched. The man was covered in tattoos; a small scar ran over one of his eyes. He looked terrifying. "It's okay, Aislinn." He said, "Just rest. I'm taking you somewhere safe."

A dream then. A painfully real dream. I floated in darkness for a while, unable to fully rest. I had no idea where my body was or even if what I had seen was real.

Two

I turned over, curling deeper into the pillows that surrounded me. I was the most comfortable I had been in years. My eyes popped open, taking in the wooden walls of the room I was in. Sunlight filtered in through white curtains; I could hear birds singing outside. It was peaceful, nothing like what I was used to. I sat up, noticing that someone had washed me and changed my clothes. I found a mirror. My short brown hair had been carefully brushed and placed in two braids. I wore a very simple white t-shirt and grey sweatpants that were just a little too long for me. Dark purple circles under my eyes drew attention away from the dark brown of my irises. In short, I was clean, but I still looked awful.

The bedroom door creaked open, and the woman from my dream stepped through. Xava was far prettier in person; her full figure was tightly wrapped in a black jumpsuit. "Oh! You're awake. I'm sure you're terrified, Aislinn, but would you like some lunch? My bond, Markus, made sandwiches for everyone." I nodded, unable to speak. I could tell this wasn't a dream, but my brain couldn't believe that I wasn't still trapped. I followed her out of the bedroom, squinting at all the sunlight streaming through the enormous windows. "Alura, close the curtains. She's not used to this much light." Xava commanded.

"Aislinn." I turned to the voice I never thought I would hear again. Everett had changed in the years we had been apart. He'd grown into his broad shoulders. His dirty-blond hair was longer, falling into his face, but what shocked me most was the milky-white color of his irises. Once upon a time, they had been the most vivid green.

"Everett?" I croaked, before I rushed into his open arms, "Oh Mother, Everett. You're alive." I wailed, tears streaking down my face.

"I've been looking for you for so long, I never thought this day would come." His voice broke, tears running down his face.

I grabbed his face, unable to stop myself from pressing my lips to his. He smiled as I pulled away, but I noticed he didn't look at me directly. "You're blind."

His cheeks turned pink, "Ah, yes. Harris' punishment for the crime of being a little too loud when you disappeared."

I felt my face drain of blood, dizziness overcoming me, "I'm so sorry." I whispered in horror.

"Whoa, it's okay, Aislinn. You didn't do it, and I handle it just fine." Everett said, rushing to pull me back into his arms, "You're worth all of the pain in the world."

"Why don't you eat something?" Xava said, reminding us that we were not alone. Xava now stood next to a willowy woman with blonde and black hair. I could see the bond pulsing between them, confusing me. Could she be bonded to more people? I'd never heard of a witch bonded to multiples. Everett gripped my shoulders, turning me back toward him. He motioned to his right, bringing my attention to a massive plate of delicious-looking sandwiches. Without a second thought, I grabbed two, scarfing the first one down in seconds. The second, I ate more slowly, aware of the eyes on me.

A blonde man entered the room, beelining to press a kiss to Xava's forehead. He then turned to me, "Hi, Aislinn. I'm Markus. I hope you like the sandwiches. Please have more. Dagger and Xava may eat like they're being starved, but we can't possibly eat all of this."

I took his offered hand, "Th-thank you. I haven't eaten well in... a long time." Sadness filled his eyes at my words, but he just smiled, pushing the towering plate of food closer to me.

Everyone chatted about mundane things while I ate, careful to keep the topics light and unassuming. I could tell they thought I was fragile. They weren't wrong, but it still caused me to bristle. "What's the plan if Harris comes looking for me?" I blurted out after swallowing the last bite of my fourth sandwich.

Xava grinned, a savage look that made me wonder what the redhead's life had been like, "Let him come. I welcome a fight."

"We will be moving to a secure location in a few days, Aislinn. I have a place." Everett said, "You'll love it, it's hidden right off the Dragon."

I grinned, remembering the days of jumping on the dirt bikes with him, flying through the Smoky Mountains along the curves. "But that's Dream coven territory." I pointed out.

"Please trust me." He said.

I nodded, falling back into silence while chatting continued to happen around me. I closed my eyes, letting my mind drift into the Astral realm. Wherever we were was hidden from the rest of the world, because I couldn't reach Harris' mind from here. I drifted, letting the quiet and peace in this place wash away years of fear. I was safe for the first time in my life. I had my bond back. Things were finally looking up.

"Well, we found more clothes in her size, but I swear Dagger was nearly arrested." A new male voice said, pulling my attention back to reality.

The man who had entered the room had black hair streaked with silver, a full beard that was just starting to turn white, though he didn't look older than his mid-thirties. His striking blue eyes met mine, and he gave me a dazzling smile, "Aislinn, it's nice to meet you finally. I'm Karson, Everett's other bond."

The bright smile on my face fell as those words filtered through my brain. Everett had another bond? That he had found while I'd been held captive... Karson was gorgeous, and from the look on his face as he gazed at Everett, he loved my bond so much.

"Aislinn?" Everett asked as I moved away. My mind was blank, I couldn't... couldn't process losing my place in his life like this. He'd probably only found me so that his power could be complete. I backed up toward the open front door, taking in all six of the people staring at me. It was too much, too many eyes.

I glanced down, noticing the keys and wallet that had been abandoned by the door. Without a second thought, I grabbed them, pumping my thin legs faster than I thought I could. I flew toward the black SUV that was parked nearby. I jumped in without a second thought, tears falling down my face as I peeled away. I didn't look back as everyone rushed out of the house. I had to get away. I could give Everett the chance to be happy with the man he loved, but I couldn't watch them love each other while I was on the outside.

I would be okay alone. I loved my solitude. I was truly free for the first time in my life; I could find my own place in the world without anyone to hurt me.

Three

Four Months Later...

I sipped my coffee, pushing my glasses up my nose as I stared at my computer screen. The article I'd been working on for the last few days had me stumped. I was lucky I was my own boss, or someone would be breathing down my neck for answers.

I was happy. Lonely, yes, but truly happy for the first time in my life. I had my own small apartment. I had started working for a small online newspaper, which had led me to start my own blog. I didn't have much, but it was all I'd ever wanted... mostly. I could ignore the occasional tugging in my chest or the pushing against the barrier I'd built around my dream world. Even if, every time, a small part of me screamed to let Everett in. Maybe I could live with a platonic bond. It was watching him love someone else completely that I couldn't bring myself to deal with. I was happy he'd found Karson. If anyone deserved their happiness, it was Everett. He'd suffered for years as part of the Dream coven. Their homophobic views had led them to torture him for years.

The sound of chair legs scraping across the floor brought me out of my thoughts. A beautiful petite woman with skin the color of mocha sat down across from me. I could feel the power rolling off of her, even if I didn't have Other sight like most witches. I tensed, closing my laptop, preparing to run.

"Let's just talk," Her accent was easy to place, but not one I'd heard often, "I know you've set up a nice life for yourself here, Aislinn. I'm just here to give you some information."

"Say what you have to say." I responded, "But can you at least introduce yourself first, since you clearly already know me?"

She smiled, offering me her hand, "Larissa De Valois, Priestess of the Shadow Coven. Xava enlisted me to help find you since I've been on the run before as well."

The information surprised me, given the confidence the woman before me carried. Why would she have ever run from anyone? Clearly, she was powerful enough to defend herself. "Nice to meet you... Hopefully." I responded.

"Harris has your location." The words caused blood to drain from my face. My hands began to shake, "We only know because Karson has been stalking his dreams. Everett wants you to join him at their safe house. He asked me to tell you..." She trailed off, "Listen, Aislinn, as one witch to another, I can see that you're terrified of this guy. I didn't press anyone for details on why you've been hiding, but sometimes we're not running from someone else. We're running from ourselves."

I cringed as she read me with no effort. I was running from disappointment and heartache. I didn't even give them a chance to talk to me. A part of me still didn't want to. I was desperate to protect what little of me that was undamaged. Now I was in danger, with nowhere to turn. I had to face my fears of yet another rejection. One that would likely destroy me.

"Thank you... For coming." I said, standing from the table, "Was there anything else?"

Larissa reached into the loose dress she wore, pulling out a flip phone, "Just call the only number in the contacts when you decide to stop running."

I dropped my bag on the floor of my apartment. It was sweltering, the AC unit was clearly on the fritz again, so I yanked off the jean shorts I wore and tossed them aside. I opened my fridge, cringing at how bare it was. I didn't really have enough money for groceries, but I usually had more than the two eggs and a carton of chocolate milk that sat on the top shelf. I bypassed both of them to grab a bottle of water, chugging it down while I paced the kitchen. I dug the flip phone out of my bag, set it on the counter, and stared at it. If Harris knew where I was, it wouldn't be long before he came to collect me. I couldn't go back to being his whipping boy. I would never help him disturb our gods. Yet facing Everett after I'd run from him felt almost impossible. How could I ever look my bond in the eyes, knowing that he had saved me, and I'd thanked him by running away.

I didn't want to be a coward, so I picked up the phone. I held my breath as it rang.

"Aislinn," Everett answered.

I cringed at the hope in his voice, "It's me. Larissa said to call you. I don't want Harris to find me."

"I'd never let that happen. Send me your address. We'll come pick you up." He responded with vigor.

I knew 'we' would be him and Karson, but I didn't let myself react. Karson was his bond as well. They cared for each other; I couldn't let my feelings affect their relationship.

"I'll be ready. Does your safehouse have WiFi? I need it for my job." I asked.

"We have everything you need, Aislinn. See you soon." Everett disconnected the call without another word. I texted the address over and glanced around the sparse space I'd made my home for the last few months. I dragged a backpack out of my closet and quickly tossed all of my clothes and small items inside. When I realized there wasn't anything else to pack, I sat down on the couch, letting myself stare off into space as my mind drifted to Harris. I thought I'd finally escaped my father. Yet here I was planning to run from him. Someday I would have to face him, but I had no power that he didn't know about. No way to defend myself against him except in dreams.

My eyes drifted shut, and slowly I fell asleep.

I sat on a cloud, my hands resting on my knees as I meditated. My dreamscape had become my favorite escape: fluffy clouds, bright blue skies, and complete silence. The barriers were still substantial as I tested them. No sign that Harris or anyone else was trying to invade my dream. I glanced up, noticing the bubbles of other nearby dreamers floating above me. The image of Larissa floated by, and I couldn't stop myself from grabbing it. My magic let me slip into her dream without any hindrance.

I blushed when I found her naked, riding a giant man with short black hair. I shouldn't have been embarrassed. I'd stumbled into so many sex dreams over the years I should be used to it, but... I was still a virgin. Larissa's head turned toward me, and the dream instantly changed.

She was now wrapped in a bright white fluffy robe. "My apologies for that, Aislinn. I wasn't expecting any visitors."

"Ah, no worries. It's completely natural," I responded.

"You called Everett." She stated, as if she'd always known I would.

"I did. I can't defend myself against Harris." I explained.

"There's more to it than that." Larissa was clearly more observant than I'd expected. "Everett seems like a very sweet guy who would do anything for you. Why did you run?"

"Everett's gay." I blurted. Larissa's eyebrows raised, but I corrected myself, "Well, he's bisexual. He always preferred men when we were younger, but when we found out we were bonded, he seemed happy. My father kidnapped me and held me captive for years. Everett found me... He has another bond... A man."

"And you don't think he can love you both?" Larissa asked.

I shook my head, "He prefers men. I can't be selfish."

"The Mother and Father don't make mistakes with our bonds. I'm actually bonded to two men." She revealed.

"Do they...?" I trailed off, unable to finish my question.

She laughed, "They're both straight, but if they wanted to, I wouldn't have a problem with it. Bonds are meant to strengthen us and our covens. Give Everett the chance to tell you what he wants himself."

I nodded, "Thank you, Larissa."

"No problem, Aislinn. We, witches, have to stick together." I pulled out of her dream, settling back onto my cloud.

Everett and I weren't children anymore. I didn't need to protect him from the bullying within the Dream coven anymore. I could accept whatever relationship he wanted with me, even if it was just friendship.

Four

Soft knocking on my door brought me out of my dreamscape. I stood, fumbling to pull my shorts on before I threw open the door. Everett and Karson filled the doorway; both looked as nervous as I felt, which made me feel strangely better.

"Hi." I waved, "I've got everything packed. Just a second."

Karson stepped forward, plucking the bags from my hands, "Come, Aislinn. Let's get you home." Something about the act made my stomach flip. It was so dominant, yet somehow still comforting. I followed behind Karson.

Everett was at my back, and I turned my head, "How do you manage without a guide dog or one of those sticks?"

"You'll meet my guide dog, Harper, later. The actual answer to your question is magic." He explained quietly as they escorted me to a white minivan. I raised an eyebrow at the choice of vehicle but didn't comment. "Most of the time, I have Harper with me, but a blind man with a dog draws more attention than I wanted. I can use my magic to slip into the Dream realm partially. I can still see there, so I'm able to move through my surroundings as if I can see perfectly."

"Wow... That's impressive. To split your mind between the dream world and the real world." I looked at him in a new light. Everett had always been in awe of my Astral projection abilities. He had considered himself weak by comparison. Anyone who could exist in between the waking and dream world was extremely powerful. Very few Dream witches ever got to that point.

Everett blushed at my compliment, before climbing into the back seat, "You take the front. I know you get car sick."

Karson glanced at me, "Buckle your seatbelt. It's a pretty long drive."

I did as he asked, and we all settled into silence as he took the turn onto Main Street. I'd been staying in this small town on the border of North and South Carolina. I couldn't bring myself to go further. Maybe some part of me hoped I'd be reunited with Everett. Plus, the town was adorable, with a population of only three hundred people. The shops were all inside historic buildings. Everyone smiled and waved at each other. Even though I had been a silent stranger, I'd been welcomed without question. I would miss it, but as I glanced at Karson's profile, I had hope that things would work out.

I was horribly bored. We'd been driving for hours, barely speaking. I sighed loudly, shuffling in my seat. Karson glanced over, "Do you need to use the restroom? There's an exit coming up."

I shook my head, "No, I'm fine. Just... How did you two meet?" I blurted out.

Everett snorted, "She's bored."

"Ah." Karson said, "I met Everett through a friend of a friend. He needed someone who could Astral project. Thought it would help in his search for you."

"Oh." I felt guilty for asking, "You can Astral project? I didn't think there were many witches who still had that ability."

"Until you, I was the only one this side of the world." He responded, "After we tried a spell, our bond snapped into place." I nodded along as he spoke. His voice was like honey, trapping me in its cadence. He glanced at me, his blue eyes meeting mine. "I hope you don't think that my bond with Everett in any way lessens what the two of you have. You both have been through hell at the hands of the Dream Coven. The connection you have is unbreakable."

"Thank you for saying that..." I trailed off, unsure if I wanted to say what floated through my mind, "I know Everett prefers men. I promise I have no intention of sleeping with him."

Karson swerved as his widened eyes landed on me. Everett choked from the backseat, "Aislinn! What are you talking about?"

Heat flushed my cheeks as hot embarrassment coursed through my body, "Well... It's just... Y'all are sleeping together. That's normal among bonded witches, but I don't... We don't have to sleep together."

"Mother, save me," Karson muttered as he took the exit. He swung into a darkened parking lot, putting the car in park before he turned his full attention on me, "Aislinn. I'm bisexual as well."

"Oh. So..." I trailed off, unsure what to say.

"Honey, if Karson and I are bonded and you and I are bonded... Most likely, you're also bonded to Karson." Everett explained.

Without a thought, I lifted my hand, magic coursing down my arm, "Let's find out." Before either man could react, my light blue magic filled the car. I laid my glowing hand on Karson's arm. Deep purple magic shot out from our joined skin, but before I could react to the bond snapping in place, I was yanked into the dreamscape.

"Aislinn." Karson's voice pulled me forward, yanking me toward a place I'd never been before. I gasped as I stepped out into rolling green hills. In the distance, I saw cows grazing peacefully.

"Where are we?" I asked.

"I don't actually know. Another place and time. This was the first place I came when I discovered my Astral projection abilities." He explained. He motioned for me to join him, so I took a seat beside him in the grass. "I come back here when I need to think."

"I can go," I said, moving to stand.

"Please stay." His voice held a tone I didn't recognize. "Did you run all those months ago because you were afraid that Everett and I wouldn't have a normal bond relationship with you?" I nodded, unable to respond, "I can't be angry with you. You'd just escaped years of captivity and abuse. I'm sure finding out your bond had bonded with another was a shock. I wish you had given us the chance to talk to you. We've wasted so much time."

"I needed the time. I needed to be my own person and learn what life outside of my father's grasp was actually like." I admitted, "I'm sorry if I hurt you or Everett when I ran."

Karson grabbed my hand, "I'm a lot older than you and Everett. I have more patience. I'm glad you had the chance to be on your own, but you never will be again."

"I think I'd prefer that," I admitted. We had leaned in closer at some point, and now Karson closed the gap, his lips capturing mine. Our kiss was electric, in this space where feelings were different, more intense. It felt like diving into the freezing ocean and soaring over mountains. When we parted, I found myself in his lap, his hands resting on my hips.

"I'm going to take you in the dreamscape very soon, but not for the first time," Karson growled, lifting me from his lap.

"I'm a virgin." I blurted out.

He stilled, glancing over me, "We're going to discuss that, but first, why don't we get back to Everett?"

I came awake with a gasp. Glancing back to find Everett staring off into space, "Welcome back, Aislinn."

I turned red as Karson turned around in his seat, "Did you know she's a virgin?"

Everett froze, glancing toward me, "I mean... It makes sense with the way her father always treated her."

"Explain," Karson demanded as he turned to me.

I sighed, "I'm Harris' bastard. My mother was not a member of the Dream coven. Just a roaming witch that had been granted refuge. Harris cheated on his wife, and she fell pregnant with me. What he didn't know was that my mother was an extremely powerful witch. She passed on her power to me."

"Where is she now?" He asked.

"Dead," I responded, emotionless. "She died before my first birthday. Harris claimed that someone had shot her after recognizing her from a dream."

"But you don't believe that?" Karson said.

I shook my head, swallowing hard. "Even if he didn't shoot her himself, which I think is completely possible. He set her up to be killed. She was a complication to his perfect image as Priest."

"I hate him." Everett hissed.

I thought for a moment. I didn't hate my father; I feared him. I wanted him not to exist, but I didn't know if that was truly hatred. Obviously, if he'd never held me captive, Everett may not have met Karson. Sometimes, horrible things had to happen to make way for great things to happen. Everything had a price. The bonds now pulsing in my chest were worth every bit of my pain. "He's not worth hating. Hate will eat you alive inside. The best thing we can do is make him irrelevant in our lives."

"He's still a threat, Aislinn." Karson pointed out. "I understand the sentiment, but we cannot pretend he isn't still out there waiting for the right moment. He fears and covets your power. That makes him dangerous."

"I know." I sat back in my seat. "Can we finish our drive?"

Karson and Everett both nodded, returning to their positions. This time, as we drove, the silence was more comfortable. When I began to fall asleep, I didn't let myself drift into my dreamscape. I fell into a deep sleep, letting myself truly rest.

Five

As the car turned off, my eyes popped open, taking in the sunrise peaking over a small brick house. I glanced over to see Karson already looking at me, "Welcome home, Aislinn."

I continued to look around, taking in the light blue shutters, a small garden full of blooming peonies, and the four rocking chairs on the front porch. It was homey, beckoning me to the bright yellow front door. "This is your home?" I asked. I smacked myself internally. It was a stupid question.

"Our home. Everett and I bought it together, with the hope that one day you'd be living with us as well." He admitted.

I was speechless at his correction, and it only made me feel worse for running away. I didn't regret it. I needed the time alone to heal and figure myself out, but I shouldn't have abandoned them without allowing them an explanation. "I'm sorry... I shouldn't have run off."

"I don't blame you, Aislinn," Everett said. "Don't apologize anymore. You did what you felt was right. So long as you're healthy and safe, I'm fine."

"But you won't ever run from us again." Karson rumbled, the look in his eyes changing, "You belong to us now, and we aren't going to let you go."

I nodded, my mouth going dry with lust. Karson continued, "What I would like to do is undress you right here, and fill you sweet virgin holes until we all pass out... Instead, I'm going to take a shower and go to bed. Just know, little dreamer, very soon I am going to claim your body as the Mother and Father intended."

With that, Karson disappeared, leaving Everett and I standing alone in the entry of my new home. "Mother, that man really does have a way with words," Everett said.

I snorted, before turning to face him, "Are you okay with all of this, really? I don't want you to feel--"

"I'm going to stop you right there." Everett moved toward me, backing me against the wall, lowering his voice. "Karson may be more dominant than me, but I have been craving your body since we were teenagers. I will be taking your pussy first."

My eyes widened, "Right now?"

"Eager little thing." He mumbled as one of his hands ran over my side, "I have an idea, but I'd need your consent first."

"Anything you want, you can have." I panted, goosebumps breaking across my skin as he continued to run his hands over my sides.

"Those are dangerous words, Linn." He breathed in my ear, "Go to the third room on the right, we designed it for you. Undress. Go to sleep. I am going to take you in this world and the dream world so that I can see every inch of your perfect body." He pressed a small kiss to my lips before stepping away.

I moved without thought, following his instructions exactly. When I opened the bedroom door, I gasped. The walls were painted a deep blue, with a mural of the night sky taking up an entire wall. The bed in the center of the room was massive, draped in light-blue sheets with white fluffy clouds. Tears filled my eyes. The room was perfect, exactly what I would have chosen for myself. I stripped out of my clothes, taking a few extra moments to explore until I found the adjoining bathroom. I rinsed myself off, ensuring that I was perfectly clean before I climbed into my bed completely nude.

It took me longer than usual to fall asleep, excitement making my heart race.

I wasn't in my dreamscape when I opened my eyes. Instead, I was lying on my back staring up at Everett. His eyes weren't nearly white here; instead, their true green stared back at me. A grin spread across my face. "You can see me here."

Everett nodded, "In all your perfect glory." I glanced down to find that I was still nude, "Don't move. I want to take a moment to appreciate your body." It was hard to stay still as his eyes roved over me. "Turn over. Get on your knees." I did as he said, gasping when his hands gripped my thighs, spreading me open even further. "I've dreamed about this pussy for years. Wondering if I'd ever have the pleasure of sinking into you." When his hands roamed down my back I tensed, remembering all of the scars my body carried, but as if he could read my mind Everett said, "You are so strong. So perfect."

"I love you." I blurted out, barely able to contain myself, "I have loved you for so long. Finally, being together is literally my dream come true."

"Mine too." He said, "Now, I am going to fill you up, make this pussy mine. I'll leave your ass and mouth for Karson."

My pussy was hot at the idea of Karson taking any of my holes. That man oozed sexual energy. I understood why Everett was attracted to him, "You like that idea, don't you? What if Karson and I kept you fully asleep, unable to drift into the dreamscape while we took you?" I whimpered at the thought of being so helpless for my bonds. Before I could respond, Everett slid a finger into me. I couldn't hold in my moans.

"Please, give me more. I can take it."

Everett laughed, "I know, Linn, but we're going at my pace. I want to explore every inch of you."

I whimpered again but didn't say anything as he added a second and third finger, hooking his fingers into a spot that caused white spots in my vision. When he pulled away, I nearly screamed from frustration, but he quickly pressed the tip of his cock to my entrance. He was wider than his fingers had been, uncomfortably stretching me. "Relax. You will take me." I forced my muscles to loosen. My core ached as he pressed into me, inch after inch, causing me to cry out. A tear dripped down my face, pain overriding pleasure. "Shh. Shh." He reached under me, rubbing one of his knuckles against my clit after he was fully seated inside me. "Father, you're so tight." As he played with me, I relaxed into his cock, pressing my hips back. He took that as his sign to begin pumping into me. Gently at first, but as my walls began to flutter with the first signs of my orgasm he pounded into my pussy. "I'm going to fill this little virgin pussy with my cum. Karson and I are going to keep you so full of seed you won't remember what it's like not to be full of our cocks."

"Yes, please." I screamed as my orgasm rushed down my spine. It was enhanced in the dreamscape, lasting for what felt likes hours. Finally, Everett grunted, filling me with his essence.

We stayed joined for a long time, though Everett turned me around wrapping his arms around my middle so I could rest my head on his chest. "Can we stay like this forever?" I whispered.

"I will never let you go again, Aislinn. I hunted across the world for you. I let you go once, but now you are finally mine." He responded.

I smiled, letting myself relax.

When I awoke in the real world, the scene was mostly the same. Everett's cock was buried inside me, my head resting on his chest as light streamed in through the sheer white curtains. I glanced to the door finding the reason I had awoken. Karson stood there, staring. "Don't move. Everett's still sound asleep. Why don't we have a little fun with him."

I grinned, loving the twinkle of mischief in his eyes. He approached the bed, carefully rearranging us so that he could see where we were joined. When he ran a finger over my clit I shivered, "So responsive. Let's wake him up the right way." I wasn't prepared for him to lean down, my leg over his shoulder, as he took my pussy into his mouth. He licked and sucked until I was squirting my release all over his face, still full of Everett's ever hardening cock. "What a good girl, squirting for the first time for her Sir."

"Sir?" I questioned.

"That is what you will call me. Soon, I will give you rules, and you'll begin to learn what I expect." He explained.

"He's a real hardass about them too." Everett said, surprising me.

"Hm. You only say that because you know I told you to wait for me to take her." Karson responded. "Don't move. I think Aislinn will thoroughly enjoy your punishment."

My eyes widened as he gripped Everett's hair, yanking his head back. He moved behind him, slapping his ass before his shoved his sweatpants down, revealing his large, curved cock. It was longer than Everett's by several inches, but not thicker. When he grabbed Everett's ass roughly, shoving himself inside I gasped at the stretch in my pussy. Karson fucked us both as he fucked Everett roughly.

The feeling was enough to send me into another orgasm, "You're not going to cum, boy. Do you understand."

"Y-yes sir." Everett responded. Karson was brutal in his pace, and I began to whimper from the ache in my core. Everett was tense, sweat dripping down his body.

When Karson finally came, my body followed as if without words he commanded me. Everett was screaming, but he had followed Karson's demanded of not finishing. "What a good boy. Slip into the dreamscape and see our perfect girl." Karson said, as he began to clean us up. When Everett slipped out of me, I sagged against the mattress completely spent.

"That was amazing." I panted.

"That was just the beginning, little dreamer." Karson said, pressing a kiss to my hair.

Six

W eeks passed in quiet, lust-filled bliss. I spent half of my days naked and boneless, one of my holes filled with one of my bonds. We ate, talked, and fucked on every surface in our small house. It was fascinating at night, most of all. Karson would meet me in my dreamscape, and we'd Astral Project to some new realm's dreamscape, exploring the universe in our dreams.

As soon as my eyes opened, I knew something was wrong. Instead of the night sky with fluffy purple clouds, I stared at the sterile white walls of my childhood bedroom. When I reached out with my mind, searching for Karson, my skin lit on fire, and a thunderclap shot down my spine, making me scream.

"You've been a very bad girl, Aislinn." Harris' voice boomed through my mind, "But don't worry, I've found your mind now. It won't be long until I get my hands on you. I've felt your power growing. I've sent your sister to deal with you. It is her right as the future Priestess of the Dream Coven."

I couldn't respond as pain raced across every inch of my subconscious. I could feel his power seeking out my memories, desperate for more information on what I could do. I'd been so careful to give him nothing all those years. Now my mind was wide open, unprotected. My thoughts were cut off as a purple light flashed across the room. The walls literally melted around me as Karson appeared before my eyes. His face was cold; his hand wrapped around Harris' neck. I gasped as my mind was released.

"You're not welcome here." Karson growled, "Father, cast out this intruder." Light blue magic flared now, Karson's brow alighting with the crown of a Priest as Harris' body began to shake violently. I felt the burn of my own Priest mark on my brow as my body moved closer, called by some ancient being.

In my mind, a male voice said, "Relax, daughter. I am here. Watch carefully." I knew instantly that the Father had answered Karson's call. He had taken control of my mind. My hand was steady as I laid it against Harris' cheek. I didn't blink as my god showed me every memory Harris had. The Father read his entire being in seconds. I could feel that he'd made it painful, forcing my father to suffer all of his worst moments again. Tears dripped down his face, but he was silent. "He is not yours to kill. Push him from your mind, build a fortress around your consciousness once he is gone, so that no one but your bonds can ever enter again. You are one of my chosen children. We will meet again."

With those words, I felt the Father fade from my mind, leaving behind so much knowledge that my head pounded. In seconds, I gripped Harris' mind, hurling him from my dreamscape with ease. Once he was gone, I turned my eyes upward, building a dome of thorns across the sky. I left only the smallest hole, a spot for Karson and Everett to always enter and entwine themselves with me.

As soon as the final pieces of my fortress were built, my eyes popped open. My mouth was dry, and my neck ached, but as I took stock of my mind and body, I found that I was okay. Even though I knew I had hundreds of extra memories and information, my brain had somehow organized them before I woke. Likely with some help from the Father.

Karson bolted upright, reaching for me in a panic. I let him pull me into his lap, "Are you okay?"

"I'm... good. I have so much to tell you." I said, squeezing his shoulders.

"I couldn't reach you. I don't even know how I got to you." He babbled.

I ran my fingers over his brow. I couldn't see the glowing crown anymore, but I knew it was there. "You're a Priest now."

"Without a coven?" He asked.

"No, with a coven that we have to save." I climbed from his lap, pulling on a pair of shorts before throwing one of Everett's tees on. "We're going into town. Get dressed. I have someone to go meet."

"Aislinn, what is going on?" He asked before I made it out the door.

"It's time you met my sister."

Karson hadn't let me out the door without more explanation, but eventually I'd convinced him we needed to head Ciera off, instead of allowing her hunt for me. Everett sat in the passenger seat while I sat in the back of the van, legs crossed, hands on my knees. My eyes were open, staring through the windshield, but I didn't see a thing. I was in my dreamscape, watching the images of my father's memories of my mother. She'd been beautiful, with long blonde hair and a golden dust of freckles across a perfectly straight nose. I only shared her warm brown eyes. I didn't have her curves, but it didn't seem to matter to Karson or Everett that I had a modest chest and broader hips. What I hadn't expected was just how much of a lie my entire life had been. She wasn't a refugee nomadic witch. She'd been the last woman of the original Dream Coven's bloodline. Harris wasn't the one with a legacy; she was. Isalyn Mairse had been married off to Harris to conceive the next heir. He'd been a powerful warlock for many years, and Isalyn's father had been charmed by his eloquence. I was not his bastard; Ciera was. He hurt my mother and killed my grandfather months after I was born. Marrying a simple servant with whom he'd been carrying on an affair. He'd moved in his inner circle and taken over the Dream Coven with an iron fist. He was Priest only by magical lies. He had no true Priest mark upon his brow. Neither did Ciera, which is why she was on her way to kill me.

I wasn't worried about that. I was going to systemically destroy everything Harris cared about, starting with her. Knowing that I had lived a lie, perpetrated by my own father, was the final straw of my morality. I was going to bathe in the blood of every person who had kept me chained my entire life. I wouldn't kill him. I had been commanded by the Father not to deal the final blow, but I would make sure he knew who had brought about his demise. I just had to be smart.

"I don't like your plan." Everett said for the seventh time, "It's too risky. You have no idea if what you're going to do will work."

"Stop trying to destroy her confidence, boy," Karson growled.

"I'm not! Why are you okay with her going into the lion's den alone?" He shouted back.

"Because Aislinn is strong. We cannot protect her if we allow her father to keep us hiding in that house forever. She needs to explore the world without fear." Karson said.

I moved, letting myself fall back into my body. I moved from my seat, placing a hand on each of their shoulders, "Pull off. Before I go, we need one last moment together."

Karson did as I asked. Before he'd put the car into park, I had stripped out of my clothes. "I want you both inside me at the same time."

"I'm taking her ass this time," Everett said before he crawled into the back.

"No... I want you both in my pussy." My cheeks burned as I admitted that. His breath hitched, but he hurried toward me.

"There's lube in the bag in the trunk. Get it." Karson commanded Everett as he pulled me toward him. His fingers were already sinking inside of me; his palm pressed against my clit. "This will hurt at first. We're both larger than average."

"I don't care." I moaned, seconds before he wrung my first orgasm from me. He pulled away just enough to slap his hand against my pussy, causing me to convulse.

"Two more," Karson commanded. Everett's hands joined in, fingers ghosting over my nipples, before he roved lower, gripping my ass. When he sank his fingers into my ass, pumping faster than I could have prepared for, I cried out.

They continued like that, sucking, slapping, and finger fucking me until I'd drenched all three of us. Then Karson commanded Everett to lie down, and I mounted him. I put on a show for Karson as I rode Everett's thick cock torturously slow. When he'd had enough teasing, he moved closer, pushing me forward. He slid two fingers inside of me, the stretch of his fingers with Everett's cock burned, but I pushed past it. Moaning as he hooked his fingers against my G-spot. Everett sucked one of my nipples into his mouth, pushing me over the edge. Before my orgasm faded, Karson began to press his cock in. I screamed as my pussy stretched beyond reason, and tears filled my eyes as the pain washed over me. My legs shook, but Karson gripped my neck, "You're a good girl, taking both of our cocks in your tiny little pussy. Sir wants you dripping with both of us."

"Please." I cried. Karson held me still as they found a rhythm, slowly fucking me together. Pleasure started to make my entire body tingle, and as Everett began to play with my nipples in time to their thrusts, I couldn't stop another orgasm from racing down to my toes like lightning.

Everett groaned, his milky eyes rolling back in his head as he came inside me. Karson's grip on me became bruising as he pumped faster, chasing his own pleasure. Within seconds, he was moaning as his seed painted my insides.

We all collapsed, panting and drenched in cum and sweat.

"I love you both." I said when I finally caught my breath, "It's been too fast, but nothing about my life has ever been normal. I am so glad the Mother and Father led me to you."

"I have loved you since the first time I laid eyes on you." Everett said, "I hate that I can't see you now."

"I will be your eyes," Karson said, "Aislinn, you are our hearts. The piece we both need to feel whole." I couldn't say anything else. I kissed them both before we all put our clothes back on.

Karson drove the rest of the way into town. We parked at a small park, and I shouldered the backpack I'd managed to put together hastily. "Before you go." Karson pulled out a small box, "We bought this for you a couple of days after we got home. I was going to wait to give it to you, but you need to have it now."

He opened the lid, revealed a delicate silver chain with a tiny cloud charm hanging from it. "It's gorgeous." I breathed as I picked up the bracelet. Karson gently took it from my fingers and attached it to my wrist.

"We're always with you," Everett said, leaning around Karson to kiss my forehead.

"You will stay safe, Aislinn. That's an order." Karson added.

I climbed out of the car, knowing there was a chance I'd never see them again. But I had to leave them behind for my plan to work. If Harris saw my bonds, he would instantly know I was coming to hurt him, but if Ciera brought me to him, I'd be on the inside.

Karson pulled off slowly, knowing he couldn't watch what was about to happen. I found a seat on a small bench and closed my eyes.

The moment I slipped into Ciera's dream, I heard her obnoxious laughter, "Big sister, to what do I owe the honor. You really are saving me time coming here. I thought I'd have to actually start looking for you tomorrow."

I didn't speak as I closed my eyes, reaching deeper into Ciera's subconscious. I dug my nails into her dream. "You will do what I say. If you're fortunate, I will let you live after Harris is gone."

I manipulated her dream until I was certain she'd do exactly what I wanted her to—implanting fake memories and dreams that would explain to her how she'd found me sleeping alone on a park bench. When I was certain that when she awoke, my plan would be in motion, I slipped from her mind.

My dreamscape awaited, inviting and safe. I settled in, disassociating from my body until the exact right moment. I'd conserve my energy until I could unleash myself on the corrupt members of the Dream Coven.

Seven

Karson

I stared at my cellphone, watching as the green dot representing Aislinn moved further and further away from me. Some instinctual part of me vibrated in rage that my bond was being taken from me. She had put herself in danger, and I had sat by and watched it happen. Thankfully, the bracelet we'd given her had a new tracking spell in the charm. So long as she wore it, she would be safe. I'd gotten the spell from my cousin Kelso; some elemental magic I didn't have the capacity to give a fuck about right now.

"We need to follow her," Everett said for the seventh time.

"They can't know we're following. We both know where they're taking her." I explained again.

Before he could respond, his phone rang. Dagger's smug tone blasted through the car speaker, "Your woman has been captured again. I thought you had her at the safe house."

"How do you know that?" I asked.

"I'm a Protection warlock, dumbass. My bonds and I laid a spell on Aislinn after we rescued her. We can't track her, but we know when she's in danger." He explained, "Want to explain how you have epically failed at keeping her out of her father's hands?"

"How fast could you meet us near the Dream Coven's property?" Everett asked, "A lot is going on, but she went in on purpose. She's going to need support."

"We'll meet you there. Six hours. We've got friends who will join us as well." Dagger hung up before either of us could respond.

"Well, we might as well get moving," Everett said.

I agreed. I needed this to be over. My bonds needed to be safe in our home, or I was going to lose my mind.

Everett and I arrived at the meeting spot early, but Xava, Markus, Alura, and Dagger were already waiting for us. I tensed as two Blood witches appeared with them.

"Karson, Everett meet Bambi and Fang. Future Priestess and Priest of the Blood Coven in Georgia." Xava introduced us.

Bambi was taller than most women, nearly nose to nose with me as I shook her hand. Her curves and long blonde hair didn't hold any desire for me, nor did the tall red-headed man who glowered at me. "Nice to meet you," Bambi said, a genuine smile on her face. She seemed kind, though all the Blood witches I'd ever met were cutthroat bitches. I didn't trust her, but I wouldn't turn down any help that would keep Aislinn safe.

"Give us the rundown on what's going on," Markus said as he clapped Fang on the back. It was clear they were well acquainted. I liked the Dovey Coven, so I would have to learn to like their friends.

"Harris invaded Aislinn's dream. There's a lot we don't know because she didn't share, but basically... She's gone into the wolf's den to kill all of the corrupt members of the Dream Coven." Everett explained.

"The Father gave her information," I added. Everyone went still at the mention of our god.

Xava sighed, "It's always something with our gods, isn't it. They haven't given us a moment's rest since we became a coven."

"They haven't even cashed in the debt we owe them yet." Alura pointed out. I tensed; a debt owed to a god was a very dangerous thing.

"You can't be complaining. They gave us everything we have now. We will continue to do what they ask of us until our dying days." Markus chastised his bonds.

Fang snorted, "We are but pawns in the games of the Mother and Father. Just be glad they give us such beautiful prizes."

I nodded. While I loved and respected our gods as any good warlock should, I knew Fang was right. We were mortal beings blessed with power, and the Mother and Father were literal gods. Whatever they wanted, they would get. I was glad to be on their side.

"Enough blasphemy. How long until we should intervene on Aislinn's behalf?" Bambi asked, getting us back on track.

"She said we'd know when she was ready for us," Everett said.

"Well, we might as well get comfortable then." Dagger sighed, taking a seat on the ground.

Aislinn

Cold water being dumped over my head pulled me out of my dreamscape. I opened my eyes, finding myself in my childhood bedroom again. The only difference is I felt no fear as Ciera sneered down at me. I stood in time to avoid a kick aimed at my head. My sister snarled in rage, grabbing for me. I reached for my powers, catching her head between my hands. "Sleep," I muttered, watching as she dropped to the ground like a sack of potatoes. I reached deeper into her subconscious, pulling her deepest fears to the surface. I set her nightmares upon her mind numbly. Once she started to groan, I stepped over her body and reached for the doorknob. Ciera was an arrogant idiot because the door opened with no problem.

I was inside the Dream Coven for the first time in years, but I felt nothing as I traversed the halls of my former home. My mind was entirely focused on my mission. I crept along silently, seeking the basement door. When I finally came to it, I took a deep breath before I descended into the damp darkness. The basement was a maze of corridors. I opened every door, but only rats, mold, and boxes greeted me. Just as I was beginning to lose hope, I heard quiet whimpers. I had to force my legs not to rush toward the sound, but as soon as I heard a muffled scream, I threw open the door they emitted from.

"We've been waiting for you, Aislinn." Harris' voice sent shivers down my spine. "I'm surprised it took you so long to get here. Ciera must have given you more of a challenge than originally expected."

I snorted, "Your bastard has always been weak. Just like you."

His face turned an alarmingly shade of red, but he didn't lunge toward me like he would have a few months ago. "I shouldn't have underestimated you. You are my daughter after all." I raised an eyebrow, refusing to engage in his mind games. "Surely, you can see why I've done all that I have. I only want to Dream Coven to be the best. The first to enter the god realm."

I rolled my eyes, "I guess you didn't learn your lesson when you were banished from my mind." He furrowed his eyebrows, and I realized he had no idea what happened. He didn't know that the Father had been there. I rushed to change the subject, "That's not why I'm here. Let her go."

Harris grinned, moving out of my line of sight. My mother lay on a thin cot, hooked up to an IV, thrashing in pain but unable to move due to the restraints holding her in place. I had no memories of her; she'd already been subdued down here once I was old enough to form memories. "Go ahead, Aislinn. Unhook her, take her wherever you'd like. She's been useless to me since you were born. She disappeared into her mind years ago. The only reason I keep her body alive is to maintain my place as Priest."

I moved to her bedside, smoothing her hair away from her forehead. She had aged a lot since the last memory Harris had of her. I laid my hand on her chest, risking everything to drop directly into her dreamscape.

It was dark, a type of darkness I'd never experienced before. Fear skittered down my spine as I began to feel my way through the blackness. I walked and walked until the darkness began to fade into a familiar basement. Feminine screams rang out; their terror and pain made my feet run to help the person. I arrived in the room, finding my mother in a thin white gown, coated in blood, and clutching a small bundle in her arms. "You will not take her from me. You can have the coven, but please leave me with my daughter."

I saw a shadow of the memory, but my mother's shrieks didn't end. When the bundle vanished from her arms and the scene began to change, I closed my eyes. I let my power flow from me. Blue light raced over my skin as I reshaped the dream. When I opened my eyes again, I stood in the only place I'd ever known peace as a child. The abandoned gardens of the Dream coven, only now they were overflowing with fruit and flowers.

"Who are you?" I turned to find my mother staring at me. When I didn't immediately answer, she circled me, her eyes moving to the crown upon my brow, "My baby." She breathed. Before I could react, she swept me into a crushing hug. "My sweet baby. My daughter." Even in the dream, her tears soaked through my shirt, but it wasn't long before my own followed. I could feel her love for me as if it was in the very air in my lungs. I had been loved and wanted. "Why are you here?"

"You deserve to be free. Our Coven deserves to be free." I pulled away.

My mother ran a hand over my cheek, "You are all that I imagined you would be. A Mairse to the very core. I am sorry that I have failed you. I was blinded by your father's charm."

"You know that you will die when I free you from this nightmare?" I asked, ignoring the tears that rolled down my cheeks.

She nodded, "I have been dead for a long time, Aislinn. Do not grieve me. I will always be with you."

"I will avenge you. I will take back our Coven. Everyone will know who he really is." I cried as I reached out with my mother, stripping Harris's magic from my mother's mind. The world shook as her body began to die; finally, her soul was already looking to exit her body. "Be free, Isalyn Mairse."

"Be free, Aislinn." Her mind echoes back to me, before I pulled myself from her dreamscape.

I was sobbing as I pulled out of her mind. Her body was still on the cot, "Look at you, Aislinn. You killed your mother. I never thought you'd become what I needed, but I think you've finally got it." Harris wrapped something around my neck, choking me. I didn't panic, letting the world turn black. I needed to recover while Harris continued with his plan. Freeing my mother from her prison had taken more magic than I had expected.

I reached out before I lost consciousness, brushing along my bonds. They were strong and bright as I faded into my dreamscape. Soon we'd be reunited.

Eight

When I came to again, I was strapped down. It wasn't an unfamiliar position to me. I'd spent many years lying on this table, staring at the ceiling of my father's office as he invaded my mind or found some new and inventive way to torture me. I didn't allow myself to react as I became aware of the people standing around me. I took stock carefully. Six men, two women, all people I knew to be involved with Harris' inner circle. I didn't think he'd make it so easy for me to wipe them off the face of the Earth.

"We know you're awake, child. You might as well be polite and greet my friends." Harris said as he strode over to me, "They're all here to see our final demonstration.

I took a steadying breath before I spat in his face, "Let them watch you die."

I didn't even flinch as he backhanded me, blood filled my mouth, but I took the opportunity to spit on him again. I knew I was playing with fire; he could kill me if he wanted to. I knew he wouldn't. He needed me.

"Come on, Harris. Let's get on with the demonstration. Don't let the stupid girl ruin our good time." Harris' wife, Anna, cooed.

He nodded, directing everyone to gather around. They joined hands in a circle around us, their magic becoming visible as they all began to chant. I'd heard the words before, but they didn't scare me as they once had. Harris might reach the realm of the Mother and Father, but he wouldn't like what he would find there.

Power flooded me as Harris gripped my arm, joining in with their chant and manipulating the power to be channeled through me.

I gave him a bloody smile just before he yanked me into the dreamscape. For just a moment, I saw the fear on his face, and I felt truly in control for the first time in my life.

Everett

I walked by Karson, allowing him to guide me through the halls of the Dream Coven. We'd moved in the moment Aislinn had given us the signal. It'd been easy enough to enter. I still had friends within the coven. They'd been more than happy to help when I'd explained that Aislinn was coming to take the Dream Coven back from Harris. He wasn't liked, but he had ruled over the Dream Coven with enough fear that no one dared to stand up to him. If I had as a teenager maybe Aislinn would have been saved all the years of torture she'd had to suffer through. My sight had been a small price to pay to be rid of Harris from my life.

I felt the stirring of intense magic, causing me to stop, "We need to find her now."

"We don't know these halls the way you do. You'll have to lead us." Karson whispered, glancing back at the Dovey's and their friends.

I nodded. Splitting the world between reality and the dreamscape was tricky, but if I did it just right, I could navigate us to my bond. The world shifted in colors of grey as I slipped into my dreamscape. While I had once been able to see in color, whatever Harris had done to blind me physically, affected what I could see here too. I moved my body jerkily, my connection to it strained from this distance. When we arrived at the door, I could see the blue magic of Dream Witches leaking out. I slipped back into my body without a thought, I didn't need to see to fight. I had trained for months to operate on only my hearing in a physical altercation.

I didn't expect Xava to step forward, "Let me go in first."

"That's a big fucking shield." Karson muttered.

"She is a Protection witch." I pointed out as we followed in after her. Shouts went up first, followed by magic zinging all around me. I left Karson's side, a scent of strong sandalwood cologne drawing my attention. "Father, I'm not surprised to find you here."

"You're no son of mine." He hissed back. He'd disowned me the moment I came out, even when I bonded with Aislinn he'd still refused to acknowledge me.

"Good. It won't be patricide when I kill you." I said seconds before his fist connected with my jaw. I didn't hardly flinch at the punch, before I was dealing my own. One after another until blood coated my hands. I was thankful I couldn't see it. When my father began to beg for his life, I snapped his neck. I had no remorse. The man had tortured me all my childhood and was now assisting in harming the woman I loved. He deserved far worse.

As I was wiping the blood from my hands off on my pants I heard Karson grunt in pain. Without a thought, I slipped back into the dreamscape taking in the room around me. Harris' wife had Karson on his knees, a knife to his neck. I moved faster than I thought I could, a well-aimed kick throwing her backward. Karson stood, pressing a kiss to my head, "Thanks for the save."

I grinned at him, "I'm just glad it's me saving you for once."

"I'll never live this down." He muttered.

I heard a female scream before Bambi said, "Everyone's been dispatched. What are we doing about... that."

I knew she was talking about Harris and Aislinn. Harris was collapsed atop my bond, his body almost completely covering her. I reached for her dreamscape, hoping to pull her out, but I found myself locked out.

"Nothing right now." I responded, "Karson and I are going to gather the other coven members. Get them on board with our hostile takeover."

"We'll watch over her." Xava said.

We gave our thanks before heading out of the house. The Dream Coven sat on an isolated compound deep in the North Carolina mountains. Very few of the Dream witches ventured out into the world. It was dangerous, because other witches and warlocks often used Dream witches for their power. As we approached the lines of houses, an older woman stopped us. "Everett Venna, it has been many years since you've walked the Dream coven's land."

"Hello, grandmother." I responded.

"I take it from all the blood; you've returned for revenge?" Her voice betrayed no fear, but that was no surprise to me. Evie Venna didn't know fear.

"I'm supporting Aislinn's rightful place as Priestess of the Dream Coven." I explained, "We've come to talk to everyone."

"Your father is gone?" I couldn't read what she wanted from me, so I nodded. She sighed, "Thank the Mother and Father. This coven has fallen into corruption ever since that bastard Harris took over."

My eyebrows raised in surprise at her words, but I said, "Can you gather everyone?"

"Wait until Aislinn is here. We all know the truth. You don't wear the Priest's mark; they won't respect what you have to say."

"I do. I will be Priest alongside my bond." Karson spoke for the first time.

My grandmother was silent, but I felt her assessment, "You are a stranger. The people of the Dream Coven have been suffering for a very long time. They won't trust your word. Come join me for tea while we wait."

We followed, but my skin itched to return to our bond. We had no idea what she might be suffering in her dreamscape.

Nine

Aislinn

Harris dragged me through realm after realm. His rage grew at every world that was not what he was looking for. I laughed as he tossed me to the ground. "Take me where I want to go."

"No," I responded.

When he moved to hit me, I ducked, kicking his knee hard enough to hear it crack. He screamed at the pain, but didn't stop his assault, "You will take me to the god realm."

"Over my dead body." I snarled.

"That can be arranged." He growled, gripping me once again. I felt his power entangle with my astral projection, but it had grown weaker. My plan was clearly in motion if his power had already begun to wane. We flashed to another realm. I didn't have time to even glance around before he was manipulating my magic for the next one. We went on like this for what felt like hours, flashing from place to place, exchanging blows, and barely stopping until finally he landed in a dark realm. Fire rolled over the land. Harris barely managed to avoid being burned alive.

I laughed, but it quickly turned into a hacking cough. Blood leaked from my lips. He was pushing my power past its breaking point. "Get up." He snarled.

I didn't move, couldn't if I was being honest. When his fingers tangled in my hair, something inside me snapped. I was tired of the games. I dragged myself off the ground, forcing him to release me. With a roar I didn't know I was capable of, I launched myself at him, pummeling him with my fists, sinking my teeth into any of his exposed flesh. When he cried out in pain, desperately trying to defend himself, I gripped his short hair. I gathered my magic, "You want to meet the gods. Fine. I'll deliver you to their fucking doorstep."

I reached my mind across the universe, finding the Father's unique signature. It had been embedded in my mind ever since he'd possessed me. With the blink of an eye, I sent us flying through the universe, realm after realm flashing before our eyes, all while I dragged my father along, screaming. When we landed on the steps of a massive black castle, with purple, starry skies stretching above us, I finally released him.

It was not the Father that stood before me, but a girl. She looked younger than me, maybe nineteen or twenty. Her white hair curled around her face, but her startling purple eyes were what made me take a step back. "Who are you?" She asked.

"Aislinn Mairse. I... uh... I'm looking for the Father. I brought him a gift."

She glanced down at my father, who had not moved from the ground. He stared up at the sky in awe, but I couldn't bring myself to care. I wanted to go home to my bonds. "He's alive." She pointed out.

"At his request," I explained.

"Daddy! You have a mortal visitor," She screamed.

For a moment, nothing happened, but when shadows suddenly formed the shape of a hulking man, I took a step back. "Thank you, Valterra."

"Whatever." She waved him off, turning back to me, "I haven't met a witch who was still alive. Wanna be friends?"

"I- Sure?" I responded, unsure what to make of the strange girl.

"Val, stop scaring the good mortals." The Father sighed, "Thank you, Aislinn. You've done a great service to me."

"What are you going to do with him?" I couldn't stop myself from asking.

"He will suffer. That is all you need to know." He snapped his fingers, and Harris disappeared. "I am sorry to tell you that your duty is not at an end. One day, the Mother and I will call on you again."

"For what?" My heart was beating out of my chest.

"Trust that I do not ask anything of my children that I have not sacrificed for." He rested a hand on Valterra's shoulder, "This is our daughter. You are the first witch to meet her. I ask that you keep her true identity a secret, but if she wishes to be your... friend. I will allow it."

Valterra squealed, "Thank you, Dad." She turned to me, "Aislinn, I'll definitely be seeing you again soon, but I know you have some people waiting for you."

I smiled, something about her was so innocent, "Can't wait. And thank you... both. It will be my honor to serve the Mother and Father in whatever way I can."

"Go home, child. Take your rightful place as Priestess with your bonds and know that we are with you." The Father swept his hands out, and everything went white.

I woke up with a gasp. "She's awake." A female voice said.

When I tried to sit up, I found that I was still strapped down. I struggled before Xava appeared over me, "You're safe. We've got you. Just stay still for a minute while I get you out of these."

She worked quickly, and before I knew it, I was sitting up. The room was a disaster; blood and bodies were littered everywhere. "Where is my father?"

"His body disappeared about twenty minutes ago in a flash of purple light." A red-headed man with a thick accent answered. When he gave me a strange look, he said, "Sorry. Fang Boucher. Future Priest of the Blood Coven."

"He's my bond." A buxom blonde said, "Bambi Cruor. Sorry, we're meeting under such shitty circumstances, but Priestesses gotta stick together."

I nodded, overwhelmed by the sheer number of strangers. I hadn't been exposed to many people outside of my father's inner circle. Even when I was free and living alone, I'd mostly kept to myself. "Where are Karson and Everett?"

"They went to talk to the Coven. We will escort you down there." Dagger said.

I stood on wobbly legs but waved everyone away as they rushed to help me. I had beaten my father. I would face my coven appearing as strong as possible. We walked through the property, and I glanced back at the house. I realized just how many horrible atrocities had been committed under its roof. I veered off to the gardening shed, the Dovey coven, Bambi, and Fang hot on my heels. I rustled through the rotting remains until I found gasoline and matches. "Burn it to the fucking ground," I instructed them.

Dagger, Bambi, and Fang grinned at me, each taking a gas can from my hands. I watched as they disappeared into the house. I took the last gas can and carefully walked around the entire perimeter, ensuring the house was soaked. Once they had all made it back outside, I lit a match and threw it in the front door. The fire started instantly, but I kept lighting matches and throwing them until the entire house was ablaze.

Laughter bubbled up in my chest, and I couldn't stop the giggles that fell from my lips.

"Aislinn?" Karson's voice had me turning around. I launched myself into his arms, ignoring the entire coven that had followed him from the safety of their homes. "You won?"

I nodded, "It's over."

"No, it's just beginning," Everett said from his left. I pressed a kiss to both of their lips before I moved to face the Dream Coven.

"I am Aislinn Mairse. Daughter of Isalyn Mairse. My entire life, I have been lied to and abused. Harris Mclain was not the rightful Priest of the Dream Coven. I have ended his rule over us all, and I have come to claim my rightful place as your Priestess." A few cheers went up from the older folks in the crowd, but I silenced them with a hand, "Rebuilding won't be easy. It will take a long time for all of us to heal, but I hope you will give me the chance to prove myself to you."

An older woman whom I recognized as Everett's grandmother stepped forward. "Aislinn Mairse. We have been waiting to hear those words for a very long time."

With her acceptance, the entire crowd erupted into celebration. We danced and laughed as the house burned at our backs. The Dream Coven was finally free.

Ten

I was on my knees, naked, waiting by the door. My mind was quiet as I waited for Karson to return. Everett sat in the same pose to my left. A birthday surprise for our bond after months of hard work. The Dream Coven was rebuilding slowly. It helped that we had been able to build bonds with the Doveys, Shadow, and Blood Covens.

When the door opened, Karson instantly spotted us, dropping his bag. "What a nice surprise. Both of my submissives are actually behaving for once."

"We are here to serve you, Sir," Everett said. I watched as he leaned forward, pressing his forehead to the floor.

Karson unbuckled his pants, "Suck me." He commanded. Without hesitation, I took his cock into my mouth, but Everett bumped against my hip. I moved, and together we licked and sucked until Karson grabbed both of us by the chin. "Bedroom. Aislinn, I want you sitting on his cock as soon as I get there."

I grabbed Everett's hand, and we rushed into the bedroom together. Once he lay back, I sank down on his cock, moaning at the stretch. I don't know that I'd ever adjust to how big my bonds were. When Karson entered, he hummed, "Look at how pretty you are all stretched out around him. Play with his nipples, he loves that." I did as he instructed, rolling Everett's nipples between my fingers roughly. He moaned, bucking into me. I saw stars as he slammed against my cervix, but I didn't stop. Karson joined us on the bed, "Neither of you are allowed to cum until I've filled Aislinn's ass. Is that understood?"

"Yes sir." We both echoed.

Karson wrapped his hand around my throat, squeezing gently before he started to press kisses down my spine. When he reached my ass, I stiffened, earning me several slaps to the ass, "Relax. You will take every inch of me."

I whimpered but did as he said. The head of his cock pressed against my entrance, and I cried out as he viciously pushed past the tight ring of muscles. While he'd been prepping me to take him, this was the first time either of them had put their cock there. He pushed more slowly when I stopped resisting.

Everett moaned, "I can feel you through her."

"Play with her clit." Karson demanded. I tensed as Everett pinched and rolled my sensitive bud, the sensations were too much. "Do not cum, girl."

"Please." I cried, "Please, please, please." There was no mercy as Karson began to fuck me harder, Everett playing with me faster.

"She's going to cum if I don't stop, Sir." Everett panted. His face was red from holding off his own orgasm.

Karson's hands slapped down against both my nipples, "Then she'll be punished."

I screamed as they both continued to fuck and torture me. I hovered at the edge of orgasm, desperate to follow Karson's command. "Look at my good girl. Filled to the brim with our cocks. Beg me for my cum in your ass."

"Please, Sir. Please, fill my virgin ass with your seed. I want you inside of my ass every night." I babbled incoherently, begging and crying for my bond. Finally, I felt his release begin, and I couldn't hold back my own orgasm a moment longer. Everett followed us both into bliss, our moans and screams blending together.

Karson carefully lifted me, pulling me in between their bodies as he laid down, "My good subs. I love you both so much."

"I love you too." I whispered just before I drifted to sleep.

I lay on a beach chair, staring up at the purple sky as Valterra told me about the most recent power she'd discovered. I'd been meeting her in various realms for months. At first, I'd done it out of respect for my gods, but now I actually liked Valterra. She had become my best friend, my confidant when I needed to complain about my bonds or my role as Priestess.

"Earth to Aislinn. Are you even listening to me?" She said, snapping her fingers in front of my face.

"Busy thinking about how wonderful you are." I responded.

She grinned, and for a moment there was silence between us. "Thank you for being my friend. I know I'm not exactly normal."

"Normal is boring, and who wants to be bored by their friends." I shot back. My mind drifted, and without thinking I asked, "What happened to my father?"

"Would you like to see?" Valterra asked, "I can take you to him."

"Really? I... Yes, I'd like that."

With a snap of her fingers, I found myself standing in an entirely new place. Still in the realm of the Mother and Father, with its purple sky hanging above us. There were no stars here, and as I looked around my eyes landed on Harris. He was thin now, his skin held a ghostly cast, but the rivets of blood that ran down his back drew my eyes.

"Aislinn?" I turned at my mother's voice, "Tell me you aren't dead."

I shook my head, "No, momma. Just visiting with a friend." I nodded to Valterra.

My mother's eyes widened, and she bowed deeply, "Princess, it is a pleasure to be in your presence."

"Your daughter is my best friend. Please call me, Valterra." She responded. "I'll leave you alone. Catch you next time, Linnie."

I smiled at the nickname she'd given me. No one other than my bonds had ever given me a nickname before, and I loved it. I glanced down, noticing the bloody whip in my mother's hand. "We take turns, Harris' victims. Every day, one of us chooses a new way to torture him. The Father comes sometimes too. He will never hurt anyone again." My mother rushed to explain.

"Are you free now? Happy?" I asked her.

She nodded, a bright smile on her face, "I watch you sometimes. You're doing a wonderful job as Priestess, better than I ever did. And those bonds of yours... You deserve every moment of happiness they give you."

We hugged. Another piece of my soul found closure as she dropped the whip, "For one night he can just think about how he ended up here. I'm going to spend time with my daughter."

We talked for hours about her life and mine. I learned about the first time she learned of her Astral Projection abilities, and I shared what few happy memories I had in my childhood.

As the sky lightened, I could feel the pull back to my body. "I love you, Momma. I'm sorry Harris took away our lives together."

"Me too, baby, me too. Just remember, he can never take away your happiness again. Go, live your life. Be free."

For all my life I'd been a caterpillar, forced into a box that my father had created to suck my power away. Now I was a butterfly, free to live the life I always wanted.

Epilogue

"Are you sure I'm dressed appropriately?" I asked Karson for the second time, smoothing the simple blue chiffon dress he'd selected for me.

"It's a bonding ceremony, Linn. Not an art gallery opening. You look perfect." Everett laughed, as Harper led us through the crowded space. Everyone glanced toward us but quickly averted their eyes when they noticed the crowns upon our brows.

"It's the first time I'm meeting Kelso, and his bond mates!" I whispered shouted.

Karson laid his hand along the back of my neck, "Relax, Aislinn." Stress instantly melted from my shoulders at his command. His dominance and rule soothed my anxiety, without making me feel trapped. I couldn't have picked a better man for Everett and me.

"Karson!" A man with brown hair and stunning blue eyes rushed to wrap his arms around Karson, "It's been too long. I'm so glad you could come." The man reminded me of an excited puppy as he turned to me, "You must be Aislinn. I'm so sorry. I'm Kelso." As I looked at him, I could see the family resemblance. The strong jawline, the eyes, even their hair was fashioned in a similar way.

"I've heard a lot about you. Congratulations on finding your bond." I said.

"Serafina is so perfect. I'm sure the two of you will love each other. I've got to get back there. It's almost time." He was nearly out of breath as he turned to run in the opposite direction.

We found our seats, Karson and Everett ensuring I was sat in between them. Harper rested her large, golden head on my knee, so I scratched behind her ears as we waited for the ceremony to start. A part of me wished that we had had a ceremony for our bonding, but I'd accepted that our relationship hadn't started off in the traditional way. Eventually, everyone found their seats as a frail older warlock stepped on the raised platform.

"Welcome everyone, the Green Coven is excited to honor our Priests as they bind their bond today." Claps and shouts followed his words, "Let's welcome, our future Priestess.... Serafina Aarden of the Elemental Coven." The woman who stepped out was breathtaking. Long, pin straight black hair flowed down her back, piercing dark green eyes swept over the crowd as a small smile graced her full lips. She was around my height, but she had curves most women would kill for. Kelso and two other men appeared on the dais as she made her way down the aisle. Soft music played, ethereal and perfectly fitting the woman who swept past. Her dress was cream colored covered in curling green vines and small pink flowers.

"Maybe we should have a ceremony." Everett whispered next to me.

Karson shook his head, "Aislinn would look gorgeous in a dress like that, but we've already dedicated ourselves."

"We could get human married." I muttered. Both men turned their heads to look at me in shock, "I know it couldn't legally be all three of us, but that doesn't mean we couldn't have the same type of ceremony."

A woman in front of us, turned glaring at us so Everett and Karson couldn't respond. The older man smiled, "The Green Coven is so happy to welcome you into our folds. I hope the Elemental Coven will feel the same way when you visit them." There was a line of tension as the Elemental Coven was mentioned again, but the warlock ignored the crowd as he turned toward Serafina and her bonds, "Kelso Yorke, Dax Jefferson, and Callum Thorpe, do you swear to honor your bond?" All three men nodded simultaneously, their eyes never leaving Serafina's face. "Serafina Aarden, do you swear to honor your bonds, and do take your role as Priestess of both the Green and Elemental Covens seriously?"

Serafina flinched at his words, but said, "I do."

The warlock opened his arms, the candles that were set up around the room lighting with orange flame suddenly. Vines erupted from the ceiling as a warm breeze drifted through the room. He produced a chalice, filling it with water before our eyes. "Drink and know that you are one." Serafina and her four men all held the cup, sipping from it as one, before each man grabbed Serafina and kissed her soundly. The crowd erupted with celebration, claps and shouts drowning out the warlock's final words.

"It really was a beautiful ceremony." I said as we climbed into the van. The drive from Virginia to North Carolina wasn't a short one, but Karson insisted he wanted to return home tonight.

"Were you serious earlier... about getting married?" Everett asked from the back seat.

Karson turned to look at me, his warm brown eyes filled with something I didn't understand. I nodded, and he wrapped a hand around my neck pulling me in for a kiss. "Making you my wife is exactly what I want." He said as he pulled away. "Buckle up."

"Really? You want to do an actual ceremony? Invite all of our friends?" I was shocked he'd agree.

"I want you to be mine in every sense of the word." Everett chimed in, "We both do."

I grinned, "Then I guess we're getting married." '

A year ago, I was locked away by my father, tortured daily, with no will to live. Now I sat in the car with both of my bonds as Priestess of the Dream Coven. I had friends, people who truly loved and respected me. That was the greatest revenge against Harris. My success and happiness.

Acknowledgements

First of all, thank you! The time you invested into reading Four Twisted Dreams is what keeps this indie author writing. I hope you enjoyed Aislinn's story, you'll be getting Serafina's very soon.

I always have to thank my husband and my family, the Cantrell Clan, first. Their support of my dreams means the world to me.

And of course, Leah and Larissa, who ensure these books and characters are pretty and that I remain sane.

Most of all I want to thank my ARC team, Cantrell's Chaos Corner. Y'all make this journey worth it. The time you invest in me and my work keeps me going.

About the author

Taila Cantrell can be found lurking in the mountains of East Tennessee with her husband. Whether she's at her day job, wrangling the feral blue-collar men, tucked into a local bookstore, or at home curled up with her many cats and two pups, she's always plotting the next story. Her readers can look forward to many genres from fantasy romance to poetry to murder mysteries there is no story Taila isn't willing to give her voice to.

In every story, Taila blends spellbinding romance with trauma, chaos, and hope. Her books remind readers that even in the darkest moments, the heart still remembers how to burn bright.

Also by

The Reclaiming Wonderland Series
Code Red
Code White: Frosted Wonderland
Blue Dreams
Emerald Knights (Coming May 2026)

The Austral Witches:
Primal Echoes
One Bloody Night
Two Shadowed Hearts
Three Little Doves
Four Twisted Dreams
Five Burnt Offerings (coming June 2026)

Mercy Valley:
Wing of the Dragon (Coming April 2026)

The Tides of Desire Trilogy w/Allena Scott
A Tide of Secrets and Storms
A Tide of Silver and Sin (coming April 2026)

Standalones
Ink and Chaos: A Poetry Collection

www.ingramcontent.com/pod-product-compliance
Lightning Source LLC
Chambersburg PA
CBHW051008050726
47592CB00007B/2760